I0623716

DECEITFUL INTENTIONS

A REVENGE MYSTERY

By

CARLO ARMENISE

Deceitful Intentions: A Revenge Mystery
Copyright © Carlo Armenise 2022

This book may not be copied or disseminated in any way, mechanical or electronic, including copying, filming, or any system for collecting and retrieving information without the full authorization of its publisher.

BantamWings Publishing
167 Madison Avenue Suite 205
New York, NY 10016
www.bantamwings.com

It is possible that any site URLs or links provided in this book have changed after publication and are no longer functional, due to the rapidly changing of the Internet. The publisher expressly disclaims any responsibility for the author's opinions stated in the work, which are not necessarily those of the publisher.

ISBN (Paperback) 978-1-958126-03-5

Printed in the United States of America

TABLE OF CONTENTS

Twenty-four-year-old Raven Redman was an orphan. When she was seventeen, her father, John Redman, died of cancer, and her mother, Alice, got killed in a car accident five years later. Raven was with her mother when the accident happened, and the car crashed at the bottom of a deep ravine. Thrown the windshield and into a tree, Raven was barely alive and drifting in and out of consciousness. As she slowly realized what had happened, Raven looked toward the wreckage to find her mother and saw Alice trapped in the car's front seat, covered in blood, screaming for help, and desperately trying to open the damaged driver's side door. Unable to move, Raven watched as the vehicle caught fire and the flames quickly engulfed Alice's body. Hearing her mother's bone-chilling screams as she got burned alive, Raven cried out. *"Mom, no,"* and then passed out.

Air-lifted to an emergency trauma center, Raven underwent a fourteen-hour surgery, was stabilized, and placed in a medically induced coma. Besides sustaining a fractured skull and several deep lacerations on her face and arms, she had multiple broken bones, including her back, and had her right leg amputated below the knee. And while the doctors did their best to repair her body, there was no way to know what the trauma to her head did to her brain.

Over the next year, after several more surgeries, they brought Raven out of the coma with a collection of metal rods and plates holding her bones together.

"Where am I?" Raven asked as she slowly regained consciousness.

"You're in the hospital," replied an attending Doctor while he examined her.

"Why?"

"You don't remember what happened?" the doctor asked.

Raven paused and tried to remember. *"No."*

"You were in a serious car accident. How about your name? Do you remember that?" the Doctor asked as he shined his penlight in her pupils.

Raven paused again. *"No, I can't remember my name,"* Raven said and started to panic. *"Why?"*

"You suffered severe head trauma, which can cause amnesia. Your name is Raven Redman."

"Raven Redman," Raven repeated her name and desperately tried to remember.

"Can you remember anything about your past?"

"My past?" Raven said. *"No, nothing. Will my memory come back?"*

"Over time, as you continue to heal, there's a good chance."

"But there's a chance it won't?" Raven questioned.

"Let's focus on the good news for now: the fact that you're alive is a miracle," the doctor remarked.

"How long have I been in the hospital?"

"A year. Your injuries from the accident were severe and required several surgeries."

Raven looked down at her missing right leg and winced.

"Is that what happened to my leg?"

"Yes. The bones were completely shattered, and we couldn't save it."

"Tell me about the accident, Doctor. Was I by myself in the car when it happened?"

"You need to rest. We can talk more later," the doctor replied, turning to leave.

"I want to know. Please," Raven insisted.

The Doctor paused, "No, Raven. You weren't by yourself. Your mother, Alice, was in the car with you. She was driving."

"Alice? My mother? Is she okay?"

"I'm sorry, Raven. She died in the accident."

"My mother's dead, and I can't remember anything about her. Do I have a father?"

"Yes, but he died from cancer a few years ago."

"Brothers and sisters?"

"No. And no other living relatives we know of."

"So, I have no family. I should have died in the accident, too," she said tearfully.

"Let me give you something to help you relax," the doctor said.

"How did the accident happen?"

"You need to recover from the coma, and then we can talk more about it."

"I'm recovered enough. Please," Raven said

The Doctor acquiesced. "No one knows for sure how it happened. They think your mother was speeding and lost control of the car somehow."

Raven paused. "What happened to her body after the accident?"

"She's buried her in your hometown. Now, rest. We need to start your rehabilitation as soon as we can."

"Rehabilitation? What's the point? I can't even remember who I am, so why would I want to get better?" she said and started to cry.

"I know it's hard, but over time, you'll heal and create fresh memories. I'll see you in the morning," he said and left the room.

"I don't want fresh memories," Raven said to herself as she laid back in the bed. "I want my old memories back."

After another year of extensive physical and psychological rehabilitation, Raven, now equipped with a prosthetic right leg, met with the hospital director.

"Your doctors tell me your recovery has gone very well, Raven. You've done an amazing job and are ready to leave the hospital," the director said with a reassuring smile.

"No. I'm not ready to leave yet," Raven said defiantly. "I don't have my memory back, and I'm still learning to walk on my prosthesis. I need to stay here and finish healing."

"I understand why you're afraid," the director replied.

"No, you don't. How can you? I'm the one who's alone and disabled, with no memory of my past. How could you possibly understand that?"

"I know your doctors have talked to you about managing your expectations when it comes to your memory; it may not come back. But you're an intelligent young woman, and the rest of your recovery will take place while you live your life and not in a hospital."

"Where will I go?" Raven asked.

"In your mother's will, she left you her house and a life insurance payout. And people who heard about your accident paid your hospital bills. So, your new life is waiting."

Raven paused, *"I don't have a choice, do I?"*

"Yes, you do. You can choose to let your current situation keep you from moving forward, or you can choose to take control of your future and create a wonderful new life, even if your memories don't come back."

Raven realized he was right. Without a past, the future was all she had left, with or without her memories. The following day, filled with apprehension, Raven left the hospital and took the long car ride back to her hometown to move into her mother's house. On the way, as she wondered what her new life had in store for her, she felt both fear and hope. Fear that her memory would never come back, and hope that she was going to a place that might help bring it back.

Alice's house was in a residential section of a small midwestern city in Michigan. It was a brick single-story with a porch and a small yard, and before Raven walked into the house, she paused and looked at the neighborhood. It was peaceful, with beautiful trees and bushes lining the street in front of a series of identical single-story brick houses. At that moment, the living room curtains on the house across the street slid open, and an older woman cautiously peered out. Raven waved, and the woman drew the curtains back again.

"*A future friend,*" Raven smiled as she picked up her suitcase and backpack and walked into the house.

Considering the house had been vacant since the accident, Raven was surprised to find it clean and well-maintained. The furniture was uncovered and dusted, and the rugs and the hardwood floors were vacuumed and mopped.

"*Looks like someone's still living here,*" Raven said as she set her luggage down in the living room and looked around.

The furniture in the room comprised a multi-colored fabric couch and matching ottoman, two overstuffed chairs covered in the same multi-colored fabric, and two hand-carved mahogany end tables. On top of one table was a handmade ceramic ashtray and a small, framed picture of Alice, a teenage Raven, and a middle-aged man, Raven assumed was her father. She picked the picture up and looked at it.

"*I hope I'll be able to remember you both someday.*"

She set the picture down and turned her attention to the living room walls adorned with several original oil paintings signed by Alice.

"*You were very talented, Mom,*" Raven said with a smile as she admired the paintings.

On the other end table near the couch, Raven saw a picture that caught her attention. It was a picture taken at a birthday party and showed a teenage Raven hugging Alice as she blew out the candles on a cake with "Happy 40th" written in frosting. Raven and her mother looked like beautiful sisters. They both had long blonde hair, piercing blue eyes, and slender, fit physiques.

"You were so pretty, Mom," Raven said. *"I'm so sorry you died."*

Setting the picture down, Raven picked up a hand-crocheted throw from the couch and draped it around her shoulders. "Thank you for this, mom. It'll keep me warm," she said as she left the living room, walked down a hallway, and into a small kitchen.

The kitchen was a vibrant yellow and decorated with various whimsical, hand-drawn cooking sketches. In the center of the room was a hand-painted wooden kitchen table with four matching wooden chairs, surrounded by a refrigerator, a stove, a sink, a pantry, and several cupboards and drawers. Raven opened the drawers and found silverware and other cooking utensils, and in the pantry, she found coffee, a coffee pot and coffee cups, drinking glasses, and a calendar hung on the inside of the pantry door.

"It's from the year of our accident," Raven said as she flipped through the calendar, tracing her finger across the several handwritten appointments Alice marked on different days of the months. *"That was a terrible year,"* Raven said, placing the calendar in a drawer and sitting at the kitchen table. *"I know we must have had a lot of wonderful talks at this table, Mom,"* Raven said as she stroked the tabletop. *"And someday, I know I'll remember them all."*

Raven left the kitchen and continued down the hallway to a bedroom she could tell was hers before the accident. The room had a bed populated with stuffed animals, a dresser, a bookcase, a small closet, and music and sports posters on the walls.

"I know these posters meant something to me before my accident, and I hope they will again," Raven said and walked into the closet.

Finding several of her clothes from before the accident, Raven touched every dress, blouse, and pair of pants and hoped one of them would trigger a memory, but nothing happened. Disappointed, she left the closet and walked over to the bookcase. On the shelves, she found high school yearbooks, photo albums, sports trophies, and framed pictures of herself and Alice at various ages and events. Raven picked up a photo of herself in a cheerleading outfit, standing in front of a college dormitory, hugging another cheerleader with their pompoms raised.

"I was in college and a cheerleader, and I've lost that too," she whispered as she set the picture back in the bookcase, picked up one of the yearbooks, and sat on the bed. *"Maybe this will help me remember."*

The book was from her senior year in high school. Flipping through the yearbook, Raven saw herself as a cheerleader, president of the student council, and as a prom queen, with her arm around a good-looking young man named Paul Manfred.

"Paul Manfred, I wonder who he is?"

A Drama Club picture with the caption 'Senior Musical, Pirates of Penzance' showed Raven dressed as a pirate, posing with a pretty, black girl named Julia Jackson, also dressed as a pirate.

"Julia Jackson. She looks nice."

After looking through the rest of the yearbook and reading well wishes from past classmates, she couldn't remember; Raven put the yearbook back and picked up a photo album. The album contained more pictures of Raven and Alice and her father lying in a hospital bed.

"Rest in peace, Dad," Raven said as she tucked the photo album back in the bookcase and walked out of the room.

She continued down the hallway to Alice's bedroom and went inside. The room had a queen-sized bed, two small nightstands, a large dresser, a make-up table, more paintings and pictures, and scattered on the bed were pieces of Alice's clothing left from before the accident. Raven walked over to the bed, sat on the bed, and picked up one of her mother's blouses.

"Maybe I'll remember your smell, mom," Raven said as she held the blouse to her nose and inhaled.

When nothing happened, she put the blouse down and picked up a photo from the nightstand next to the bed. It was a picture of Raven in her high school graduation cap and gown, hugging Alice and laughing.

"Looks like we were happy, Mom. I want to remember those times," Raven said, yawning. *"But now, I need some sleep."*

Raven took the picture, went back to her bedroom, removed her prosthesis, got into bed, and covered herself with the throw.

"Goodnight, Mom," Raven said, looking at the picture as her eyes grew heavy. *"And thank you for the house. It's beautiful."*

The following morning, Raven was awakened by the disruptive calls of the front doorbell. After taking a moment to clear her head, Raven got out of bed, attached her prosthesis, put on a pair of jeans and a sweatshirt, went to the door, and looked through the security peephole. Standing on the porch, Raven saw an older, dark-haired woman. She opened the door.

"Can I help you?" Raven asked.

"You don't remember me?" the woman asked.

"I'm sorry, I don't. A car accident I was in affected my memory."

"My name is Muriel Manfred. I was a friend of your mother's. I came over to offer my condolences."

"Thank you, Muriel, that's so nice of you. Please, come in," Raven said and held the door open.

"How do you like the house?" Muriel asked as she walked in, and Raven closed the door.

"I love it. But I was surprised to find it so well-maintained."

"Once we knew you were coming back, a few of the teachers from the high school and I came in and freshened the place up. I hope you don't mind?"

"No. I appreciate it. Would you like a cup of coffee?"

"If you're making some anyway."

"It's already made. I set the timer last night. Let's go to the kitchen," Raven said and Muriel, trying not to stare at Raven's prothesis, followed her into the kitchen.

While Raven took out coffee cups and set them on the kitchen table, Muriel looked around.

"Your mother was a talented lady," Muriel said, admiring the kitchen sketches.

"She was. I wish I could remember her," Raven said as she brought the brewed coffee to the table and sat down.

"What do you mean?"

"I don't remember anything about my life before the accident, including my mother."

"So, you don't remember how the accident happened?"

"No."

"Will your memory come back?"

"The doctors don't know. It might not."

"Well, you should know how loved your mother was. The entire city donated for her funeral," Muriel said.

"I wish I could have been there."

"The local newspaper said you were still undergoing treatment and couldn't have visitors. That's why none of us came to see you."

"That's okay. I wouldn't have known if you had; I was in a coma for a year. And when I woke up, I had this."

Raven pulled up her pant leg and showed Muriel more of her prosthesis.

"I'm sorry," Muriel said.

"But I'm getting around on it pretty good," Raven remarked, trying to lighten the mood.

"Please, sit down," Raven said as Muriel sat down and Raven poured the coffee.

"I hope you take your coffee black. I don't have any milk. I haven't gone to the grocery store yet," Raven said.

"That's fine. I'm lactose intolerant anyway." Muriel said smiling.

"So, you were a friend of my mother's?" Raven asked as they drank their coffee.

"Yes. I teach science at the high school, and your mother and I spent a lot of time together."

"And you said there were articles in the local newspaper about our accident?"

"That's right, a couple."

"Did you save them?"

"Yes, as a remembrance."

"Can I see them?"

Muriel paused for a moment. "It was such a terrible accident. Why read about it?"

"The articles might help bring my memory back. Were there pictures of the accident scene?" Muriel cradled her coffee cup nervously and didn't answer. "Don't worry, Muriel, you can tell me. I can handle it."

"Yes, and pictures of you and your mother."

"I want to see them," Raven pleaded. "Please, Muriel."

"You're sure?"

"Yes."

"Okay, I'll bring them over later," Muriel said and glanced at her watch. "Well, I need to get home. Thanks for the coffee."

"You're welcome."

Raven escorted Muriel back to the front door.

"Please thank the other teachers for helping with the house."

"I will. And here's my phone number, in case you need something," Muriel said, handing Raven her business card. *"I'll see you later."*

"Thank you, Muriel."

Later that afternoon, Muriel brought the newspaper articles to Raven, and she sat on the couch and read through them. The accident scene pictures that accompanied the articles showed Raven on a stretcher with a body bag lying on the ground next to a burned-out and demolished car.

"Oh, my God!" Raven exclaimed as she inspected the pictures.

The articles detailed the accident and included statements from the city's Chief of Police, Ronald Manfred. He reported the car, driven by fifty-five-year-old Alice Redman, with her daughter, twenty-two-year-old Raven Redman in the passenger seat, went over a cliff and crashed at the bottom of a ravine. Alice Redman died in the crash, while her daughter survived but would probably die from her injuries.

"I almost did," Raven said, responding to what she read.

They also quoted Manfred saying that after careful inspection, it was determined there was nothing mechanically wrong with the vehicle that could have caused the accident. The brake and steering lines were still intact and working properly, and the tires showed no signs of defect. And because Alice Redman's autopsy found no alcohol or drugs in her system, it was alleged Alice must have been speeding and lost control of the car.

"I wish I could remember what happened," Raven said as she held her hands to her head in frustration. *"Please, come back."*

Raven finished reading the articles and spent the rest of the day unpacking and going to a neighborhood grocery store near the house to get food. While she shopped, a couple of older women recognized her and walked over.

"You're Raven Redman," one of them said.

"That's right," Raven replied.

"I'm Beverly Thomas."

"And I'm Susan Cook," the other woman said.

"It's nice to meet you both," Raven replied and shook their hands.

"We knew your mother," Beverly said. "She was such a sweet lady. You have our condolences."

"Thank you," Raven said. "How did you know her?"

"She was my daughter's art teacher at the high school," Beverly replied.

"My son's too," Susan replied. "Our kids loved your mom. She was a great teacher. But you know that. When did you get back to town?" Susan asked.

"Yesterday," Raven replied.

"It was a terrible accident," Susan said. "How are you feeling?"

"I'm still healing, but I'm fine," Raven replied.

"Well, it's good to have you back," Beverly said. "And I'm sure we'll see you again."

"I'm sure you will," Raven replied with a smile as the ladies walked away.

Raven finished shopping and got in line at the cashier to check out.

As she did, a teenage girl wearing a cheerleading outfit approached her.

"You're Raven Redman, aren't you?"

"Yes. Do I know you?"

"My name is Rebecca Epstein. I'm on the high school cheerleading squad. You're, like, a cheerleading legend!"

"A legend? Me? Why?"

"Because the tricks you did when you cheered for the school are still famous. Can I take a selfie with you to show the other cheerleaders?" Rebecca said as she took out her cellphone.

"A selfie?" Raven asked.

"A cell phone picture of yourself. You've never taken one?"

"I don't have a cell phone."

"Here, I'll show you."

Rebecca moved close to Raven, took the selfie, and then showed the picture to Raven. *"See?"*

"Wow, That's great."

"When the other cheerleaders see this, they're going to be so jealous," Rebecca said. *"Do you think you could come to one of our cheerleading practices and teach us some cheers?"*

"I don't remember how to cheer anymore, and I couldn't anyway," she said as she pulled up her pant leg and showed the girl her prosthesis.

"That must have hurt."

"It did, but it doesn't anymore."

"I can't wait to show this picture to the other girls. We're all so glad you didn't die in the accident."

"Yeah. Me too."

"Goodbye," the girl said as she excitedly walked away.

"Goodbye," Raven replied and took her groceries home.

That night, as Raven made dinner, she thought about meeting Rebecca and smiled. *"I can't believe I'm a legend; I needed to hear that."*

After dinner, Raven took the family photo album from her bedroom into the living room and sat on the couch.

"These pictures represent my life, and someday I know they'll help me remember."

As she looked through the pictures, the doorbell rang again. Raven looked through the peephole and saw a young black woman holding a backpack standing on the porch. Raven opened the door, and the pretty woman, Raven's age, came into full view. She was thin and fit, had short hair styled in cornrows, wore jeans with fashionable holes, and a t-shirt stenciled with the words Perfect Cut Salon – 'A good head is a terrible thing to waste on a bad haircut.' She had a peace tattoo on the back of her right hand, and the backpack she carried had a pink breast cancer ribbon pinned on the front. Before Raven could say a word, the woman walked in and hugged her.

"Oh, my God! I'm so glad you're back. I missed you so much. How are you feeling?"

"Do I know you?" Raven said, pulling away.

"What do you mean? It's me, Julia. We're best friends."

Raven paused as the recollection hit her. *"That's right, Julia Jackson. I saw our picture in a high school yearbook. We were in a Drama Club together and performed in Pirates of Penzance."*

"Yeah, that was a terrible musical," Julia groaned, then smiled. "But we had fun!"

"I'm sorry I don't remember you, Julia. The accident affected my memory."

"Don't worry. I'll bring you up to speed. I came to the hospital to see you a couple of times, but you were in intensive care," Julia said as she walked over to the couch and sat down.

"Yeah, for almost a year," Raven said, shutting the door and sitting next to Julia on the couch. *"You and I are best friends?"*

"Absolutely. Before your accident, we were always together. I'm so sorry about your mom."

"Thank you. Did you know her?"

"Are you kidding? We talked to her all the time. She was like my second mom."

"What did we talk about?"

"Everything. From boys to…, well, boys," Julia said, smiling. "She was so proud of you for being in college and studying to be a high school art teacher like her."

"I was studying to be a teacher?"

"Yeah."

Raven smiled. *"What about you? What did you study in college?"*

"I studied business, but I didn't graduate. My mom got breast cancer and needed my help, so I quit, got my cosmology license, and opened my beauty salon here in town. It's called The Perfect Cut, and that's why I wear these," Julia said and pointed at her t-shirt. *"They're my advertising campaign. Catchy, huh?"*

"Yeah," Raven said, smiling. *"Is your mom okay now?"*

"No, she passed away a year ago."

"I'm so sorry. What about your dad?"

"The fucker walked out on us when my mom got sick, and I haven't heard from him since." Julia paused as she realized. *"Sorry for the language. I only cuss occasionally, for effect. Is that okay?"*

"Fuck, yeah," Raven said, smiling. *"But you don't miss not having him in your life?"*

"Nah, we never liked each other. He said I was mouthy, and I said he was a god damned coward. Besides, I like being on my own."

"I guess we have that in common, too."

"Don't worry. You'll get used to it. Where did you get these?" Julia said as she picked up one of the newspaper articles off the coffee table.

"Oh. A teacher friend of my mom's brought them to me."

"You mean 'muffins,' Muriel Manfred?"

"Yes. But why do you call her muffins?"

"Oh, that's just a nickname I gave her. Because she's always making her crappie muffins for the teachers at the high school. If you want my opinion, Muriel and her husband are both assholes."

"Who's her husband?"

"Ronald Manfred. The Chief of Police."

"Oh, that's right. I saw his name in the newspaper. Why is he an asshole?"

"Because he runs the police department like it's his private militia. And he's also the father of your old boyfriend."

"Old boyfriend?"

"Paul Manfred. He's a cop too."

"Paul Manfred. I saw our prom picture in the yearbook. We were together?"

"Oh, yeah. You guys were hot and heavy before your accident," Julia paused and looked at Raven's prosthesis. *"I'm sorry, I didn't mean to bring it up."*

"It's okay. You can talk about it. I'm better now. At first, I was angry and felt sorry for myself, but with the help of the doctors at the hospital, I'm learning to cope."

"And I'm so glad you are."

"What about you? Do you have a boyfriend?"

"No, I'm playing the field. It's more fun. Besides, I haven't met Mr. Right yet, just Mr. Right Now," Julia said smiling. *"But you were Miss Popular in high school. You were President of the student council, homecoming queen, and Captain of the cheerleading squad."*

"I saw that in the yearbook too. But I didn't see your cheerleading picture."

"No, I wasn't a school spirit groupie; I was more interested in being unique and speaking my mind. That's why I dress like this. Do you like it?"

"I do. Except for the holes," Raven said, smiling.

"I know," Julia said, returning the smile, "Who would have thought holes in your pants would be a fashion trend?"

Raven laughed. "Did you read the articles about our accident?"

"Yeah. I know they say your mother was speeding and lost control of the car, but she was an excellent driver, so there must have been something else wrong."

"I want to remember."

"You will, and I'll help you," Julia said.

"Thank you, Julia."

"Listen, when I found out you were coming back, I canceled all my appointments for the week so we could spend time together."

"That's great. I need to get a car, but at the moment, I don't have the courage to drive."

"Don't worry. I'll drive you around until you're ready. And I already have a few places I want to show you that I know you'll remember."

"Sounds great."

"Then I'll pick you up tomorrow morning. I've got to go pick up some cat food for Martin Luther."

"You named your cat Martin Luther?"

"Yep. Doctor King was one of my heroes, and so is my cat," she said as she walked to the door with Raven.

"Thanks for coming to see me, Julia. And for being my friend."

"I prayed you'd be okay, and you are," Julia said as she hugged Raven and left. *"I'll see you tomorrow."*

The next day, when Julia came to pick Raven up, she was wearing the same holey jeans, but a different Perfect Cut t-shirt stenciled with the phrase 'The only thing worse than climate change is a bad haircut.'

"So, where are we headed?" Raven asked as she got in Julia's car.

"You'll see," Julia replied, smiling.

Julia drove Raven through the city to a cemetery nestled on a hillside. The large, beautifully landscaped cemetery was the perfect tranquil resting place, and as Julia parked near the cemetery entrance, Raven looked out the window.

"This is so beautiful, but why are we here?" Raven asked.

"I thought you might want to pay your respects to a couple of people buried here."

"Who?" Raven asked.

Julia paused. *"Your mother and father."*

"Both my parents are buried here?"

"Their graves are up the path on the right. Tell them I said hi."

"You're not coming?"

"No, this is your time. I already spend a lot of time here visiting my mom," Julia said.

Raven got out of the car and walked up the path that separated the two sides of the cemetery. At the very end of the path, Raven found her parent's graves next to each other. There were two tombstones with similar inscriptions - 'Alice Redman, wife of John Redman and loving mother of Raven Redman', and 'John Redman, loving husband of Alice Redman and father of Raven Redman.'

"Even if I don't remember the two of you," Raven said. *"I'm sure you were wonderful parents. Rest in peace."*

Raven paused for a moment and looked at the graves, pondering the situation, then walked back to Julia's car and got in.

"Are you okay?" Julia asked.

"Yeah. It made me sad to think both my parents are dead, but it's hard to grieve over people you don't remember."

"That'll change."

"I hope you're right."

"I am, I know it. Now, before we go to the next place, are you hungry?"

"Starving."

"Me, too. And I know the perfect place to get something to eat."

Julia drove Raven to the heart of the city to a local diner called The Food Oasis. The restaurant was a fifties soda shop replica, complete with tables and cozy booths, counters with stools in front of a small kitchen, and walls decorated with fifties memorabilia.

"The name of the place is lame," Julia said as they walked in, *"but this was our favorite hang-out spot in high school."*

"I can see why," Raven replied, smiling as she looked around.

"Yeah, right? Come on. I'll take you to our favorite booth."

As Julia and Raven walked through the crowded diner, the customers stared and whispered.

"Don't mind them," Julia said protectively. *"They're ignorant."*

"Don't worry; I'm used to it," Raven said as they sat down in a booth and picked up a menu. *"So, what would we have?"*

"Cheeseburgers, shakes, and fries. Especially the shakes."

"We had cheeseburgers, shakes, and fries for breakfast?"

"For breakfast, lunch, and dinner."

"No kidding? I liked their milkshakes that much?"

"Oh, yeah. I called you Little Miss Milkshake because you had so many."

As the women shared a laugh, a pretty dark-haired waitress, Raven's and Julia's age, walked up to the table with two glasses of water.

"Hi, Raven, how are you?" the waitress asked as she set the glasses down on the table.

"I'm sorry, do we know each other?" Raven asked.

"I'm Maryann Perkins. We were on the cheerleading squad together in high school."

"I'm sorry. My memory hasn't been so great since the accident."

"It was terrible, but I'm glad you're okay. And I'm sorry about your

mom."

"Thank you."

"Can we order, please?" Julia said, interrupting their conversation.

"Sure. What would you like?"

"We'll have two cheeseburgers, two chocolate shakes, and two orders of fries," Julia replied.

"No problem," Maryann said, writing the order and walking away.

"Why were you so rude to her?" Raven asked.

"Because she's a bitch. While you were in the hospital, she and Paul got engaged."

"I appreciate you looking out for me, Julia; I do. But I wasn't around."

"I know, but she's still a bitch."

"Tell me about mine and Paul's relationship before my accident," Raven said.

"You guys were inseparable. Paul was a star basketball player, and everyone thought you two would get married."

"What did my mother think of Paul?"

"She liked him, but she wanted you to go to college before you guys talked about getting married, and Paul didn't want to wait."

"Paul didn't go to college and play basketball?"

"He wasn't good enough to get a basketball scholarship, so his dad talked him into staying here and becoming a cop."

"Were we together while I was in college?"

"No. Paul got mad and broke up with you when you left for college. That's when he started screwing around with Maryann. I think he was trying to get even with you for leaving."

"Sounds like we weren't supposed to be together."

"Right. You're too good for him."

"Thank you, Julia. But at the moment, given everything that's happened, I don't feel too good."

"You will after you have your shake," Julia said, smiling.

After breakfast, Julia and Raven left the restaurant and returned to the car.

"Well, was I right about the restaurant?" Julia said.

"Yeah, it's great. And the shakes are unbelievable."

"But it didn't bring back any memories, huh?"

"No, but it was still fun. Where are we headed now?"

"To two other places, I know you'll remember."

Julia drove Raven outside the city to a park on the banks of a river and parked near a swing set and slide.

"This park is so pretty," Raven said. "Why did we come here?"

"Come on. I'll show you," Julia said as she got out of the car, walked over to the swing set, sat in one of four swings facing the river, and swung. Raven sat in the swing next to Julia's and met her pace.

"I brought you here because when we were in high school, this *was our special place. We came here just about every day to talk and figure things out until you went to college."*

"What would we talk about?" Raven asked.

"All kinds of things. Going to college, working, getting married, having kids."

"We talked about getting married and having children?"

"You did. You wanted to have a family and a relationship like the one your mother and father had."

"My father," Raven said, looking at Julia. *"Tell me about him."*

"He was great. He taught economics at the local junior college, and he loved you to pieces. Called you his princess."

"I saw a picture of him in the hospital."

"That was a tough time for you. Like my mother, his cancer was aggressive."

"I want to remember him."

"You will. Come on," Julia said, getting up from her swing and walking back to the car.

"Now, where are we going?" Raven asked, following her.

"To another place. I know you'll remember. Our old high school."

"But it's Saturday, isn't the school closed?"

"Yeah, but I know a way to get in. You up for it?"

"As long as we don't end up in jail."

"I can't promise anything," Julia said, smiling.

Julia drove to the high school, an old brick structure designed in the sixties, and parked near a padlocked back door.

"Ready?" Julia asked.

"The door has a padlock on it," Raven replied.

"Not for long. Come on."

The two got out of the car and walked to the door. After surveying the area to ensure no one else was around, Julia pulled a metal nail file out of her backpack and started to pick the lock.

"Where did you learn to do that?" Raven asked.

"I've locked myself out of my apartment a few times," Julia replied.

"Isn't there an alarm on the door?" Raven asked.

"I guess we'll find out."

Julia removed the lock, opened the door, and waited to hear an alarm ring. When they didn't hear an alarm, Julia led Raven into the school, *"Come on."*

"What if we get caught in here?" Raven asked.

"Don't worry. No one's here on the weekends. Follow me."

Julia led Raven down an interior hallway of classrooms with walls covered with sports and school event posters.

"This school is where we spent every day for four years. Remember anything?"

"No," Raven replied as she looked at the posters.

"Let's check out some of our old classrooms," Julia said and led Raven into one of the empty classrooms.

"What class did we have in here?" Raven asked, looking around the room.

"We had algebra with Mrs. Winslow. I didn't like her."

"Why?"

"Because she made me do algebra," Julia said, laughing. "But she was one of your favorites."

"She was?"

"Oh yeah, you loved her. You said she reminded you of your mother. And she thought you were terrific."

"What did she think of you?"

"She thought I was a rebel. And she was right," Julia said, smiling and walking to a desk in the front of the classroom. "This was your desk. You always sat in the front."

"What about you? Where did you sit?"

"In the back by the door so I could be the last one in and the first one out," Julia said.

"You were a rebel."

"I told you."

Raven sat at her old desk and looked around the classroom.

"Remember anything?" Julia asked.

Raven shook her head in disappointment, "No."

"Come on. I'll show you your favorite place in the entire school."

Raven followed Julia into the school's gymnasium and saw several Fighting Falcons championship banners hanging from the ceiling.

"This is where you cheered," Julia said.

"We were called the Falcons?" Raven asked as she looked at the banners.

"Yeah. Original, huh? We should've been called the Birdshits, considering how crappy we were. Come over here."

They walked over to a trophy display case with several basketball trophies and framed game photos aligned in rows.

"Look at this," Julia said, pointing to a photo.

Raven looked at the picture and saw herself dressed in a cheerleading outfit, standing on the top of a six-person cheerleading pyramid.

"That was you in our Senior year, cheering at the championship game. We lost, but you were great."

"I met one of the current cheerleaders at the grocery store, and she called me a cheerleading legend."

"You were."

"It would be nice to I remember that."

"Don't worry. It would be better to remember a game we won. All right, since the gym isn't bringing back any memories, I've got one more classroom to show you that I know you'll remember."

The two women walked out of the gym and into another empty classroom down the hall.

"What class did we have in here?" Raven asked.

"We didn't. This was your mom's old classroom."

"My mother's classroom?" Raven asked as she looked around the room.

"Yep. We were here with her every day," Julia said.

Raven walked over to the teacher's desk, sat down, placed her hands on the top of the desk, and traced the wood with her fingers. Suddenly, Raven had a memory. She remembered her and Alice sitting in the house at the kitchen table talking.

"Don't be gone too long, Raven," Alice said. "We need to leave for the college right after I get the oil changed at Dunlap's."

"Don't worry, Mom, I'll be ready."

Alice grabs at her stomach in pain.

"Ow."

"Is it your stomach again, Mom?"

"Yes. I made an appointment to see Doctor Kim about it tomorrow."

"Good," Raven said as she walked out of the kitchen, and the memory faded.

"Oh my God!" Raven said, rubbing the desktop again, hoping to get the memory back.

"Are you okay?" Julia asked, concerned.

Unsure the memory wasn't just a figment of her imagination Raven took a moment to regain her composure before she answered.

"Yeah, I'm fine. But I am getting tired."

"Let's take you home; the school's not helping you remember anyway. Sorry," Julia said as they left the school, got back in the car, and drove Raven home.

Raven stayed silent on the ride, preoccupied with the memory, and as she started to get out of the car when they got back to her house, Julia stopped her.

"I know you're disappointed you didn't remember anything, but are you sure you're all right?" Julia asked.

"Yes. And thank you for taking me to all the places we saw; they were great even if I didn't remember them."

"I'm not giving up," Julia said and took Raven's hand. *"We'll get your memory back. Hey, how about we see a movie tomorrow? I know you haven't seen one of those in a while."*

"That sounds great. See you tomorrow," Raven said as she got out of the car and walked into the house.

That night, while she was lying in bed, Raven replayed the memory repeatedly in her mind, trying to figure out if it was real.

"Was it real? And if it was, why did I have that memory?" Raven said as she yawned. *"I'll sleep on it, and maybe I'll remember more tomorrow."*

The following afternoon the doorbell rang, and Raven went to the door expecting to find Julia but instead saw a middle-aged gray-haired man dressed in a police uniform carrying a manila envelope.

"Hello, Raven. I'm Chief Manfred."

Raven remembered his face from the newspaper. *"It's nice meeting you, Chief. What can I do for you?"*

"I'd like to talk to you for a minute. Can I come in?"

"Sure," Raven replied as Manfred walked into the house, and Raven shut the door behind him.

"We've met before," the Chief said. *"Do you remember?"*

"No, I've had memory problems since the accident." Raven replied. *"When did we meet?"*

"When you and Paul were dating. He was on the high school basketball team, and we met at the games."

"Would you like a cup of coffee, Chief?" Raven asked.

"No, thanks, I can't stay. I just came over to offer my condolences. Your mother was a great lady."

"Did you know her?"

"When you're the Chief of Police in a small city like this one, you get to know everyone. She was special, well-liked. How are you doing?"

"I'm feeling better."

"It was a terrible accident. You're lucky to be alive."

"I've been told that, but I wish I could say the same about my mom."

"I know. I'm sorry. Muriel told me she gave you some newspaper articles about your accident."

"That's right. I asked to see them. I thought they would help me

remember what happened that day."

"Did they?"

"No. The articles didn't have any information about how the accident happened."

"That's because nobody knows how it happened. You and your mother were the only two people there. I brought the police report we did on the accident for you to see. I thought it might give you a clearer picture of what we do know. Would you like to see it?"

"Yes."

"I have to warn you, though - it's graphic."

"Thank you, Chief, but I'll be fine."

Manfred handed her the envelope.

"After you go through it, come by the police station and see me if you've got questions."

"I will."

"All right. Well, again, you have my sincere condolences," Manfred said, opening the door. *"And, welcome back."*

"Thank you, Chief."

After Manfred left, Raven sat at the kitchen table and opened the envelope. Inside was a three-page written report and several eight-by-ten color pictures of the accident scene and the demolished car. As the Chief said, the photos were graphic and showed Raven lying on a stretcher with Alice's body in a body bag on the ground.

The written report detailed what the police knew about the accident and said a local mechanic named Herman Dunlap was the one who inspected the car after the accident and didn't find anything mechanically that could have caused the accident. The car's brakes and steering were functional, and the tires had no defects. And although the highway pavement was dry, skid marks on the road showed that the car swerved a few times before going over a cliff and crashing at the bottom of a ravine. The force of the crash threw Raven Redman, Alice's twenty-two-year-old daughter, through the windshield and into a tree, while Alice Redman, the fifty-year-old driver, was burned to death when the car caught fire.

"Oh, my God! My mother was burned to death," Raven gasped.

The report went on to say that Raven, in critical condition, was air-lifted to a local hospital, while Alice's corpse was taken to the city morgue and autopsied by the city's Medical Examiner, Doctor Steven Simon. Since he found no drugs or alcohol in Alice's system and no abnormality or disease in any of her organs, he was able to autopsy; it was determined Alice Redman was speeding and lost control of the car, just as the newspaper reported.

Frustrated she couldn't remember, Raven looked at the photos of the car again. *"How could they make such detailed claims about the car's brakes and steering when it's just a hunk of burnt metal?"*

At that moment, there was a knock at the front door, and Julia rushed in, backpack in hand, wearing hole-less jeans and another Perfect Cut t-shirt stenciled with the phrase, 'Your soul might belong to God, but your haircut belongs to me.'

"Coffee, I need coffee," Julia exclaimed as she went to the kitchen.

"I just made a fresh pot," Raven said and followed Julia into the kitchen and sat at the table while Julia poured herself a coffee and sat down.

"Oh man, I can't get my eyes to focus until I've had my morning jolt

of caffeine," Julia said as she sipped the coffee and savored the jolt. *"Ah, that's better. What are these?"* Julia asked as she pointed to the photos of the accident.

"They're from the police report about our accident. Chief Manfred dropped it off."

"Did it say anything different than the newspaper? That your mother was speeding and lost control of the car?"

"No, but it did give the name of the mechanic who inspected the car. His name is Herman Dunlap. Do you know him?"

"No, but I do know where his shop is."

"Although he reported there was nothing mechanically wrong with the car, I still want to talk to him. Can we go see him and then go to the movie?" Raven asked.

"Sure. Now that my caffeine has kicked in, I'm primed and ready for an adventure," Julia said, laughing as she took one last swig of coffee, grabbed her backpack, and followed Raven out of the house.

When they got to Dunlap's Repair Shop, a thirty-year-old male mechanic wearing a Dunlap Body Shop uniform greeted them.

"Hello, lovely ladies," the man said, making eyes at Raven. *"Welcome to Dunlap's. What can we do for you?"*

"We'd like to see Herman Dunlap," Raven replied.

"He's in his office in the back of the shop," the mechanic said. *"Go on back. And after you see him, come back and see me. I've got a sale on tools you might be interested in,"* he said, winking unabashedly at Raven.

"Tools, huh? Like what? A limp screwdriver?" Julia said and blew

him a kiss as she and Raven walked out.

"I wish I could do that," Raven said.

"Do what?"

"Be bitchy."

"Don't worry. Professor Julia will show you the ropes."

When Raven and Julia walked into Dunlap's office, an older female secretary greeted them.

"Can I help you?"

"We'd like to see Herman Dunlap," Raven said.

"Aren't you Raven Redman?"

"That's right. Do I know you?"

"No, but I read about your accident and recognized your face from the newspaper. But I thought it said you died?"

"I did," Raven replied sarcastically. "Can we see Mr. Dunlap, please?"

"Just a minute," the receptionist said and walked into an interior office.

"How was that, Professor?"

"Not bad. But you have to sneer a little when you say it," Julia said.

A moment later, the woman returned, "Go on in." she said.

"Thank you," Raven sneered, and Julia gave her an approving nod, as they walked into the office.

Inside they found a balding, fat man in his sixties wearing a grease-stained body shop uniform, sitting at his desk, chewing tobacco and holding a coke can.

"Can I help you, ladies?"

"Are you Herman Dunlap?" Raven asked.

"That's me. What can I do for you?"

"My name is Raven Redman, and my mother, Alice Redman, was killed in a car accident two years ago and according to the police report, you inspected the car after the accident."

"Alice Redman. I remember. That car was in terrible shape."

"Yes, it was. But in the report, you said there was nothing wrong with the car's brakes or steering that could have caused the accident. Is that right?"

"If that's what I said in the report," he replied as he spat tobacco juice into the coke can.

"And you didn't find any other mechanical problems with the car?"

"If they aren't in the report, then I didn't find any."

"But how could you tell? The car was just a ball of burnt crumpled metal," Raven said.

"Lady, I've inspected hundreds of cars in worse shape than that and never had trouble finding problems if there were any," Herman replied, spitting again. *"It's what I do for a living. It's also why the police have me do their inspections."*

"And you couldn't have made a mistake?" Raven asked.

"Look, I'm sorry your mother died," he said to Raven as he spat again. "But I've been a mechanic for forty years, and I don't make mistakes."

"What happened to the car after you inspected it?" Julia asked.

"The cops took it to the city junkyard and destroyed it. Look, I'm swamped, so unless you ladies need a mechanic, I've got to get back to work," he said, getting up from the desk.

"I just have one more question," Raven said. "Do you remember my mother bringing that car in for an oil change the day of the accident?"

Dunlap paused before he answered. "No."

"Are you sure? Did she ever bring her car to you for service?"

"Just once a long time ago, but not for an oil change."

"No, huh? Well, thanks for your time," Raven said as she gave him a suspicious look and walked out of the office.

"Yeah, thanks," Julia sneered and followed Raven.

As soon as they left the office, Dunlap made a phone call.

"Raven Redman was just here asking about the oil change I did on her mother's car and the inspection report I did for the police. I think she knows something. We need to talk. And remember, if I go down, you go down with me," Dunlap said, hanging up the phone and spitting again.

On the way back to Julia's car, Raven thought about the conversation with Dunlap. "He seemed certain there wasn't anything wrong with the car that could have caused the accident."

"And he made me certain of something else," Julia said.

"I'll never spit again as long as I live. Why did you ask him about your mother having the oil changed?"

"I didn't tell you, but when we were at the high school in my mother's classroom, I thought I remembered something."

"You did? What was it?"

"I remembered my mother and me talking in the kitchen on the morning of the accident. She told me she had to get the oil changed at Dunlap's before she took me back to college."

"Wow. So going to the high school did help you remember," Julia said.

"If the memory's real. But according to Dunlap, she didn't have the oil changed, so I must have imagined it."

"Or you are getting your memory back, and Dunlap's wrong."

"Or lying," Raven replied, lost in thought.

"Hey, let's get something to eat and go see that movie," Julia said, trying to lighten the mood.

"Sounds great. But only if we can go back to the Food Oasis for another shake," Raven said, smiling.

"My sentiments exactly, Miss Milkshake," Julia replied, laughing.

That night, when Raven got home from the movie, she went into the kitchen, took out the calendar she found in the pantry and sat at the kitchen table.

"My memory had to be real," she said, opening the calendar to August, the month of the accident. On the 15th of the month, she found an appointment Alice made -'oil change - Dunlap's – 9 A.M.' And on August 16th, she found another appointment – 'Doctor Kim – stomach pains - 1 P.M.'

"My mother was supposed to get an oil change at Dunlap's on the morning of the accident and then see a Doctor Kim the next day about her stomach pains. That means a piece of my memory is coming back," she said as she closed the calendar. *"But why this piece?"*

The next day when Julia came over, Raven brought out the calendar.

"The memory I had at the school wasn't my imagination; it was real," she said.

"How do you know?"

"This calendar was from the year of our accident, and my mother used it to keep track of all her appointments," Raven said, opening the calendar to August and showing it to Julia.

"See, on the day of the accident, my mother had an appointment at Dunlap's to get the oil changed."

"That means you are starting to get your memory back. That's great!"

"I know. But why did I have that memory? And why did Dunlap lie about the oil change?"

"Maybe he just forgot. He breathes a lot of fumes."

"Maybe, but I want to talk to him again. My mother also said she was going to see a Doctor Kim about the pains in her stomach. Do you know her?"

"Sure. Doctor Kim was my mother's doctor too, so I saw her a lot when she was sick. You know her, too."

"I do?"

"Yeah, her daughter Lisa was on the cheerleading squad with you, and Doctor Kim would come to watch the basketball games."

"Can you take me to go see her?"

"Sure. I'll call her office and let them know we're coming," Julia said as she took out her cellphone. "You need to get one of these."

"I will when I can remember people to call," said Raven, smiling.

When Raven and Julia got to Doctor Kim's office, a middle-aged nurse welcomed them.

"Raven, it's so good to see you," the nurse said.

"I'm sorry, I don't remember you. I lost my memory in the accident."

"My name's Linda, and I've known you and your mom since you were a baby. I'm so sorry about your mom."

"Thank you, Linda," Raven said. "Julia told me Doctor Kim was my mother's doctor."

"Yes, and yours, too."

"And mine, too," Julia chimed in.

"That's right."

"Is she available? I have a question I'd like to ask her."

"Yes, she's expecting you. Come with me."

"You want me to come with you?" Julia asked Raven.

"I'm sorry, Julia, HIPAA laws only allow immediate family during appointments that divulge medical history," Linda replied.

"I understand. Good luck," Julia said to Raven.

Linda led Raven to an inside doctor's office and knocked.

"Come in," a woman's voice said from inside.

The nurse opened the door, and Raven walked into the office. Doctor Kim, the fifty-something, sophisticated-looking female Chinese doctor, got up from her desk.

"Thank you for seeing me, Doctor," Raven said, walking over and shaking her hand.

"Of course. You look well. Please sit down," the Doctor said and sat back at her desk while Raven sat in front of the desk.

"I'm sorry about your mom."

"Thank you."

"I read about your leg. How are you feeling?" the Doctor asked.

"Physically, I'm feeling much better. But I also lost my memory."

"Amnesia can be a side effect of severe head trauma, but there's a good chance your memory will come back in time."

"That's why I'm here. I want to ask you about a memory I did have."

"Certainly."

"I remembered my mother complaining of stomach pains the morning of our accident and saying she was going to make an appointment to see you about it. Can you tell me if she made that appointment?"

"Let me check," the Doctor said and looked at her computer.

"Yes. It looks like your mother did make an appointment about her stomach. But since she didn't come in, I have no idea what the problem was. Why are you asking?"

"Because, according to the medical examiner, her autopsy didn't show anything wrong with her stomach."

"It could have been something that wouldn't show up in an autopsy, like stomach flu."

"I understand, but at least now I know for sure there was something," Raven said as she stood up to leave. "Thank you for your help, Doctor."

"It's good to have you home, Raven, and we need to get you in for a physical."

"I'll set it up with Linda. Thanks again."

Raven and Julia left the office and went back to the car.

"So, what did the doctor say?" Julia asked.

"She confirmed that my mother did make an appointment about her stomach."

"No, kidding. Just like you remembered."

"Yeah. So, before we go back to Dunlap's, I want to talk to Doctor Simon, the medical examiner, about my mother's autopsy."

"I know where his office is; he did my mother's autopsy too."

"Great. Let's go."

"I just hope he's not in the middle of someone, I mean, something when we get there," Julia replied smiling.

When they arrived at Doctor Simons' office, a secretary greeted them.

"Can I help you?"

"My name is Raven Redman. My mother, Alice Redman, was killed in a car accident two years ago, and Doctor Simon did her autopsy. I'd like to talk to him about it," Raven said.

"Just a minute, and I'll see if he can see you," she said and picked up a telephone.

"Doctor Simon, Raven Redman is here to talk to you about Alice Redman's autopsy. Yes, sir."

"You can go in," the secretary said as she hung up the phone.

"Thank you," Raven said as they walked into the office.

Doctor Simon, the grey-haired sixty-year-old medical examiner, got up from his desk and walked over.

"It's good to see you again, Raven."

"Have we met before?" Raven asked.

"Yes, at the high school. Your mother was my daughter's art teacher, and I met you a few times when I came to the school."

"Sorry, I don't remember," Raven replied.

"I read about your memory loss. Sorry. Who's your friend?" the doctor asked, looking at Julia.

"My name is Julia Jackson," she replied.

"You're Helen Jackson's daughter. I'm sorry about your mom, too."

"Thank you."

"Please have a seat," Simon said, sitting back at his desk while the two women seated themselves.

"I want to offer my sincere condolences about your mom, Raven."

"Thank you."

"So, you don't remember the accident?" Simon asked.

"No."

"It's probably for the best. It was terrible."

"Trust me," Raven said, showing him her prosthesis. "I know. But I'm not here about the accident; I'm here to talk about my mother's autopsy."

"What would you like to know?"

"In the police report, you said you didn't find abnormalities or *disease in any of my mother's organs."*

"That's right. Besides being severely burnt and damaged by the force of the accident, her internal organs were healthy."

"Her stomach included?"

"Yes. Why are you asking?"

"Because I did remember the day of our accident and my mother complaining of stomach pains, and her doctor, Doctor Kim, verified she made an appointment to see her about it."

"I know Doctor Kim; she's great. And I'm sure she told you several things can cause stomach pain that wouldn't show up in an autopsy," Simon replied.

"I know, like stomach flu," Raven replied.

"That's right."

"I'm not questioning your findings, Doctor, but I'd like to see the autopsy report for myself," Raven said

"I'm sorry, Raven, I can't show it to you. Since your mother's autopsy was part of the investigation into your accident, the police sealed it, and I can't release it unless Chief Manfred says it's okay."

"I understand. Then I guess I'll talk to the Chief," Raven replied.

"Is there anything else I can do for you?" Simon asked.

"No. Thank you," Raven replied, and she and Julia stood up to leave.

"Again, I'm sorry about your mom," Simon said. "And I'm glad you're doing well."

"Thank you again, Doctor," Raven replied as they walked out of the office and back to Julia's car.

"What do you think?" Julia asked.

"That I still want to see the report," Raven replied.

"Then it sounds like we're headed to the police station to talk to Manfred?"

"But first, I want to go back and talk to Dunlap."

"Yeah. Let's go force the bastard to tell us the truth about the oil change and then cut his hair."

"What hair?" Raven said and the two women laughed.

When they got back to Dunlap's shop, several police cars and uniformed officers, including Chief Manfred and his good-looking twenty-five-year-old son Paul, were standing around a body bag in the center of the shop's parking lot. Paul saw Raven and walked over. Paul wasn't just handsome; he was athletic and in great shape and carried himself with all the swagger of a young cop.

"Hi, Raven," Paul said. "It's good to see you. You look great. And you, too, Julia."

"Sure," Julia sneered.

Raven remembered Paul's face from his yearbook picture.

"Thank you, Paul. You look good, too." Raven replied. "What happened?"

"Herman Dunlap's dead," Paul replied.

"What? Oh my God!" Raven exclaimed.

"How did it happen?" asked Julia.

"It was a hit and run," Paul replied.

"Hit and run in his parking lot? That's bizarre," Julia replied.

"Why would someone kill Herman Dunlap?" Raven asked.

Before Paul could answer, Chief Manfred walked over.

"Hi, Chief," Raven said.

"Hi, Raven. Julia. What are you ladies doing here?"

"I came to talk to Dunlap," Raven replied.

"About what?" the Chief asked.

"About an oil change, he did on my mother's car the day of our accident that he said he didn't do."

"How do you know he did the oil change?"

"I had a memory. I remembered my mother telling me that she was getting the oil changed at Dunlap's that morning. And then I found a note she made about having it done. But since Dunlap said he didn't do it I came back to talk to him about it."

"So, you're getting your memory back?" the Chief asked.

"Just this one memory so far," Raven replied.

"Well, as you can see, Herman's not talking to anyone, and since this is an active crime scene, you ladies need to stay back," he said and started to walk away.

"Wait, Chief," Raven said. *"I need to talk to you about something else."*

"Not now. I'm in the middle of a murder investigation. Come and see me at the station tomorrow," the Chief said and continued walking. "And Paul, remember, you're working."

"Yes, sir, I'll only be a minute," Paul replied, turning to Raven. "It's great that you're getting your memory back."

"Only a piece of it," Raven replied.

"Listen, Raven, can I talk to you in private for a minute?" Paul asked.

"About what?"

"It's personal," Paul replied looking at Julia.

"Do you mind, Julia?" Raven asked.

"No. I'll wait in the car," Julia replied, giving Paul a dirty look as she went back to her car.

"So, what's going on, Paul?"

"Well, first, I wanted to tell you how sorry I am about your mother."

"Thank you."

"And I'm sorry for not coming to see you in the hospital after the accident. That was wrong of me."

"It's okay. You wouldn't have been able to see me anyway; I was in pretty bad shape. Besides, according to Julia, at the time of my accident, we weren't together."

Paul paused. "She's right. We broke up when you left for college."

"From what Julia told me, you broke up with me."

"Yeah, I guess I did," Paul said.

"Then you had no reason to visit me in the hospital. Listen, I appreciate you apologizing, Paul, but don't worry, I don't remember anything about our relationship. And as I understand it, you're engaged to Maryann."

"I know, Julia. But I hope we can still be friends."

"We'll see," Raven said. *"Is there anything else?"*

"Yes. Something happened while you were away at college. Something you didn't know about."

"What?"

Paul took a deep breath. *"Our parents had an affair."*

Raven paused. *"My mother and your father had an affair?"*

"That's right."

"How do you know?"

"I overheard my dad telling my mother he wanted a divorce because he was in love with another woman and wanted to be with her."

"But your mother told me she was friends with my mom."

"They were until my mother found out your mother was the other woman."

"Did you ask your father about the affair?"

"Yes. He said he and Alice were in love and planned to get married after his divorce. But then the accident happened and your mother died. And since then, my parents have been trying to put the affair behind them."

"I still can't believe it," Raven said.

"For a while, I couldn't either. But I asked my mom, and she told me it was true. And now that you're back, I thought you should know."

"Thank you for telling me, Paul," Raven said. "Is there anything else?"

"Yes. Would you consider having dinner with me sometime so we can catch up?"

"What about Maryann?"

"She'll understand. It would just be dinner with a friend, right?"

"I'll let you know. Good-bye, Paul," Raven said as she walked back to Julia's car and got in.

"So, what did the chump want to talk about?" Julia asked.

"He told me that my mother and Chief Manfred had an affair while I was away at college."

"He did?" Julia asked.

"Yes. But you already knew about it, didn't you?"

"I heard rumors," Julia replied.

"So why didn't you tell me?"

"Because I didn't believe it, so I thought it wasn't important."

"Not important?" Raven said, getting upset. "Anything about my past and my parents is important to me and might help bring all my memories back. Besides, if it's true, it means my mother had an affair with a married man and may have ruined a marriage."

"I'm sorry I didn't tell you."

"Is there anything else that you felt was 'unimportant' that happened that you haven't shared with your supposed 'best friend'?"

"No. And again, I'm so sorry."

"I'll ask the Chief about the affair when I see him tomorrow. Listen, Julia, now that we can't talk to Dunlap, I'd like to go home and get some rest."

"Absolutely. I've got some errands to run myself. Let's go."

On the ride back to her house, Raven couldn't stop thinking about the affair and didn't talk.

"It's so weird that Dunlap was murdered in his parking lot. Right?" Julia said.

"Yeah," Raven replied, wanting to cut the conversation short.

"Do you think Dunlap had something to do with the accident? And that's why he lied about the oil change?" Julia asked as she parked in front of Raven's house.

"I don't know," Raven said as she got out of the car. "Thanks for going with me today, Julia. I'll see you later."

"Okay. And again, I'm sorry."

Raven didn't respond and walked into the house.

4

Still thinking about the affair, Raven went into the kitchen and took out the calendar.

"If my mother did have an affair with the Chief, there'd be something about it on the calendar," Raven said as she sat at the table.

She scanned through the months before the accident and didn't find any mention of the Chief. However, the week before the accident, there was a note about Muriel: 'give Muriel lesson plans on Monday morning before we leave for the college and thank her for the muffins.'

"Julia's right; she is Muffins Muriel Manfred. But since there's no mention of the Chief, maybe Paul was wrong, and the affair didn't happen. I'll find out tomorrow," she said and put the calendar back in the drawer.

At that moment, Julia walked into the house out of breath, carrying an armful of newspapers.

"Help," Julia said as she dropped the papers on the floor.

"What are those?" Raven asked.

"A peace offering. My mom saved the local Sunday newspapers and read and re-read past issues. She said it took her mind off her cancer. So, to make up for not telling you what I heard about the affair, I want to give you these and let you read about everything that went on in the city during the two years you were in the hospital. That should trigger some memories. What do you think?"

57

Raven took the newspapers, set them on the coffee table, and pulled Julia into a warm embrace.

"Thank you. But you don't have to make up for anything. You didn't cause my memory loss, and you weren't responsible for my mother having an affair. But you're right. Reading about the past might help me remember."

"Or make you glad you forgot," Julia said, chuckling. *"So, are we going to see Chief Manfred tomorrow about the autopsy report?"*

"Yeah, but I feel guilty that you have to drive me places."

"Are you kidding? We're partners, and I want to help. Besides, I don't have to drive you around - you can drive."

"What do you mean?" Raven asked.

"If you're going to be driving again at some point, you'll need to practice. So, I'll pick you up in the morning, and you'll drive us to see the Chief."

Raven paused as she considered it. *"All right. It's a deal. And thanks again for these,"* Raven said, looking at one newspaper.

"You're welcome. See you in the morning. I love you," Julia said and hugged Raven.

"I love you, too," Raven replied, watched Julia drive away, and then went to bed.

When Julia came to pick Raven up the next day, she was dressed in a pair of dress slacks and a plain t-shirt without The Perfect Cut logo.

"You're not wearing your Perfect Cut marketing shirt?" Raven asked as she got in the driver's seat of Julia's car.

"No. Today I wanted to be a little more conservative. "Are you ready to drive?"

"I've been thinking about this, and I don't know if I can do it," Raven said as she clutched the steering wheel.

"I understand. I'll drive."

"No. I need to do this," Raven replied. "I can't be afraid forever."

"Right. And don't worry, I'm here," Julia said as she handed Raven the car keys. "Just put the key in the ignition next to the steering wheel, start the car, shift into drive and go. I have faith in you."

"That makes one of us," Raven said as she cautiously pulled away from the curb.

When they got to Police Headquarters, Raven parked the car as Paul returned from patrol and parked next to her.

"Hi, Raven," Paul said, getting out of his car.

"Hi, Paul," Raven replied as she and Julia got out.

"You guys here to see the Chief?"

"Yes," Raven replied.

"Come on; I'll take you in," Paul said and escorted the two women to the station entrance.

"How's the murder investigation going?" Julia asked.

"We don't have any suspects yet, but we'll find out who did it. It's a small city."

'I hope you're right," Raven said. "It's a little unnerving to think there's a killer on the loose."

"What's the matter? Don't you ladies have faith in your local law enforcement?" Paul asked, smiling.

"Not all law enforcement. Just certain ones," Julia said.

They walked into the station, and Paul escorted them to a visitor's seating section.

"Wait here, and I'll let the Chief know you're here," Paul said and walked over to an office labeled Chief Manfred, knocked on the office door, and went in.

"Don't look now, but I think someone still has feelings for you," Julia said to Raven as they sat down.

"Don't be ridiculous. He's engaged. Besides, I thought you didn't like him."

"I don't, but I don't like Maryann more," Julia replied, smirking.

Paul came out of the office and walked back to Raven. "My mothers' with him, but you can go in."

"Thank you, Paul," Raven said.

"You're welcome," Paul smiled and walked away.

"Come on," Raven said to Julia.

"No. I think it's better if I wait here."

"Don't be ridiculous. We're partners, remember?" Raven grabbed Julia's arm and pulled her up. "And I need your support." She escorted Julia over to the office door and knocked.

"Come in," the Chief said from inside the office.

Raven and Julia walked into the office and saw the Chief and Muriel sitting together at a small conference table.

"Hi, Muriel," Raven said.

"It's good to see you again, Raven," Muriel replied.

"This is my friend Julia."

"Hi, Julia. Weren't you in my senior science class?"

Julia forced a smile as she remembered how much she hated the class. "That's right. It's nice seeing you again."

"I hope we're not interrupting anything, Chief?" Raven asked, gesturing at Muriel.

"No. I know you're here about your mother's autopsy report."

"You spoke to Doctor Simon?"

"He called and told me you remembered your mother complaining about stomach pains the day of the accident."

"That's right."

"Oh, are you starting to get your memory back?" Muriel asked.

"Not all of it, just this one memory," Raven replied. "But I know my mother made an appointment with her doctor about her stomach pains, and I want to know why the autopsy didn't find anything."

"Doctor Simon went over the report after you left his office and confirmed there was no disease or abnormality in Alice's stomach. But I told him it was okay to take you through the entire report and answer any questions. He's expecting you to come to his office tomorrow morning at ten."

"That's great. Thank you, Chief," Raven said.

"Is that all?" the Chief asked, an eyebrow raised.

"No. I think Herman Dunlap lied in his inspection report about there not being anything mechanically wrong with my mother's car that could have caused the accident."

"What makes you say that?" Muriel asked.

"Because he lied about doing the oil change," Raven replied.

The Chief cleared his throat. "Maybe he didn't. Maybe he did the oil change and forgot. He does a lot of oil changes. Look, Herman was the best mechanic in the city and conducted inspections for us all the time. So, if he said the brakes and the steering were working properly and there was nothing else wrong with the car, I believe him. But to prove it to you, I'll have the car brought back here to police headquarters and have it inspected again by one of our mechanics in front of you."

"What do you mean?" Raven replied. "Dunlap told me the car got destroyed after the inspection."

"That's what we told him. But after the inspection, we kept the car at the impound and forgot about it."

"So, the car can be inspected again," Muriel said. "That's lucky."

"I'll set it up and let you know," the Chief said to Raven. "Now, is there anything else? I've got a murder to solve."

"There is one more thing," Raven said nervously. "But it's private."

"No problem," Muriel said as she got up from the conference table. "I've got to go home and make muffins for school tomorrow. I'll see you at home, Chief. Goodbye, Raven, Julia."

"Goodbye, Muriel," Raven and Julia both said as Muriel left the office.

"I'll wait for you in the car," Julia said to Raven and left the office.

"Now, what's this private matter?" the Chief asked once they had all left.

"I have a question for you. And I need you to be honest with me."

"Okay."

"Did you and my mother have an affair?"

The Chief paused. "Yes. Your mother and I started seeing each other while you were away at school."

"Why didn't she tell me about it?"

"She wanted to wait until the time was right. Until we were both sure."

"Did you love each other?"

"Very much. She was an incredible woman," he paused, dwelling on a pane of light on his desk. "Who told you about the affair?"

"Your son. He told me you were divorcing Muriel to be with my mom."

"Muriel and I were getting a divorce before I met your mother and asked her to marry me."

"How did Muriel take it when she found out?"

"Not well. She felt betrayed and hated us both. But then the accident happened, and Alice died, and a year later, Muriel and I reconciled and have been trying to make it work ever since. But it's hard when you lose someone you truly love," the Chief paused again. "Does that answer your question?"

"Yes," Raven said, standing to leave. "And thank you for being so honest."

"I have no reason to lie. Your mother was very special, and it was a privilege to have even known her. And that's the truth."

"Thank you again," Raven said as she walked out of the office.

When Raven got back to the car, she sat in the driver's seat.

"So did the Chief admit the affair?" Julia asked.

"Yes. He told me that he and Muriel were getting a divorce before he met my mother and fell in love. So technically, his marriage to Muriel was already over."

"So, you feel better?"

"I wouldn't say better. I feel sorry for the Chief; he really loved my mother."

"Listen, since we're not going back to see Doctor Simon until tomorrow, how about we go to my salon and let me work a little bit of Julia magic on your hair. Trust me, you can use it," Julia said, smiling with a mischievous glint in her eyes.

"Okay, but only if you promise not to make me look too wild," Raven said, returning the smiling.

"You can trust me," Julia said, laughing.

Following the meeting at Police Headquarters, Muriel went home and began making muffins for school. As she took a fresh batch out of the oven and set them on the kitchen table to cool, the Chief walked in, took a seat at the table, and picked up one of the hot muffins.

"Ouch," he said as he dropped the muffin.

"Don't eat those. They're for the teachers. And some for Raven. I think she'll like them."

"I'm sure she will," the Chief said as he picked up the muffin again and took a bite.

"It's great she's getting her memory back," Muriel said.

"Yeah."

"What did she have to talk to you about? That was so private."

"It was just something else about Herman's accident report. Nothing important."

"Why aren't you at the station?" Muriel asked.

"I came home to change my shirt. I'll be working late again tonight."

"How's the investigation going? Any leads?"

"Not yet," the Chief said as he got up from the table. *"But the investigation just started. I'll see you tomorrow morning,"* he said, then kissed Muriel goodbye and walked out of the kitchen.

"Goodbye," Muriel said as she placed another tray of muffins in the oven. *"Yes, I know Raven will enjoy these."*

That afternoon when Raven and Julia got back to the house after her haircut, they stayed in the car to talk.

"So, do you like your hair?" Julia asked.

"I told you, it's fantastic. You're a magician with a pair of scissors," Raven replied.

"Thanks. Although I have to admit, it was easy with a client like you. Anyway, I'll be here at nine-thirty tomorrow morning so we can be at Simon's office at ten."

"And I'm still driving," Raven said and got out of the car. "And I love my haircut!" she shouted as Julia drove away.

Walking up to the front door, Raven saw a small basket of muffins covered in saran wrap with a handwritten note that read, "Enjoy, Muriel."

"That was nice of her," Raven said.

After taking the muffins into the house and setting them on the kitchen table, Raven paused, "I think I'm ready to go through your things, mom."

Raven went into Alice's bedroom, sat at the make-up table, and looked at the various cosmetics and other personal effects lying on the tabletop, including a medium-sized jewelry box.

"I know all these things will mean more to me when I get my memory back," Raven said as she opened the jewelry box.

Apart from a few jewelry pieces, Raven found a small diary. "My mother kept a diary," Raven said as she looked through the pages of the diary and found several references to her mother's relationship with the Chief.

"She was seeing the Chief," Raven said as she read a few of Alice's comments.

On September 3rd, Alice wrote,– 'Today, Chief Manfred (Ron) came to the high school to handle a disturbance. I'd met him briefly when he and Muriel attended school events, but we got to know one another today. He told me about the marital problems he and Muriel had and that they were separated and getting a divorce. I told him how much I had missed John since his death, and he understood how I felt. The conversation was natural and made me feel good. He's a good man.'

November 10th – 'Ron called and asked to take me to dinner as friends. I want to go, but it's not right. His divorce isn't final. So, I'll say no.'

February 3rd – 'Ron keeps calling and asking to take me to dinner. He says his divorce will be final this week. Even though I feel guilty about hurting Muriel, I think I'll say yes.'

March 2nd – 'I was with Ron again last night. We've been together every night for a while now and have been having such a wonderful time. I think I'm falling in love with him. His divorce is final, and he's already talking about us getting married. But I still feel so guilty when I'm around Muriel; I need to talk to her about it.'

August 15th - 'Ron asked me to marry him tonight, and I said yes. But I want to talk to Raven before we make it official. I'll do it when I take her back to college.'

August 24th – 'The pains in my stomach have gotten worse. I need to see Doctor Kim. It feels like either stomach flu or food poisoning, but since all I've had to eat is some homemade chicken soup and one of Muriel's muffins, it must be stomach flu.'

Raven closed the diary. *"Huh, food poisoning?"*

Raven set the diary back in the jewelry box and picked up a white hospital admission wristband with 'John Redman' printed on it. As she paused and looked closer at the band, she had another memory.

In the memory, her father was in a hospital bed with tubes and machines connected to his body, and a fourteen-year-old Raven and a fifty-year-old Alice were standing next to his bed.

"*The Doctor thinks the results of your last tests show improvement, sweetheart,*" Alice said.

"*Yeah, dad,*" Raven said. "*That's great news, don't you think?*"

Before John can respond, he coughs violently.

"*Are you okay, Dad?*" Raven asked as she moved closer to him.

John stops coughing and looks at Raven and Alice, smiling with deep affection embedded in his weakened gaze.

"*Thank you both for the words of encouragement, but we know the news isn't good. I love you both so much. And once I'm gone, I want the both of you to go on living your own lives the best you can.*"

Raven hugs her father, sobbing.

"*Don't say that, Daddy. You're not going anywhere. You can't. Promise me. Promise me,*" Raven pleaded.

"*You're a special young lady, Raven, and I want you to have a wonderful life - you deserve it.*"

Raven continues to sob and hold her father as the memory fades.

Distressed by the memory, Raven looked at the wristband again, "*Rest in peace, my sweet father.*"

Raven put the wristband back in the jewelry box, got up from the make-up table, sat on her mother's bed, and looked around.

"*I'm grateful I'm getting some of my memory back, but I want to remember everything,*" she said and went back to her bedroom.

As she got ready for bed, she saw the newspapers Julia gave her lying on the floor next to the bed. Raven sat on the bed, picked up one of the papers, and read the headline. 'Tommy Summers wins fifth-grade spelling bee' *"Julia's right, I did miss some important stuff,"* she said, smiling as she laid down.

The following morning, Raven drove Julia to Doctor Simon's office, and on the way, she told Julia about the diary and the memory of her father.

"My mother kept a diary," said Raven.

"What?"

"I found it in her bedroom. She wrote about the relationship she had with the Chief. She verified that she and the Chief were going to get married."

"It's too bad they didn't," Julia said.

"Yeah. And I had another memory."

"No kidding? What?"

"I remembered my mother and me being in the hospital right before my dad died. It was terrible. He was so weak."

Julia clutched Raven's hand, *"Are you okay?"*

"Yeah. I just wish I could remember everything about him."

"You will. You're getting pieces of your memory back, so it's just a matter of time."

"I hope you're right," Raven said and then drove to the appointment with Simon.

When they got to Simon's office building and started to walk in, Paul walked out.

"Hi again, Raven," Paul said. *"You must be on your way to see Doctor Simon about your mom's autopsy. My dad told me."*

"Yes. Why are you here?" Raven asked.

"I came to pick up the autopsy report on Herman."

"I thought you already knew how he died," Julia said.

"Not really. It looks like he was killed by a hit-and-run, but the killer could have just made it look that way."

"You mean he was killed before he was hit by the car?" Julia asked.

"It's a possibility. We'll know more after we review his autopsy results."

"Well, good luck, Paul," Raven said.

"Thank you," he replied with a kind smile. *"I'll see you both later."*

As Paul walked away, Julia beamed like a giddy schoolgirl. *"Oh yeah, he's still in love with you."*

"Just stop," Raven said. *"Come on; we're going to be late."*

They went into the building to Simon's office and were greeted again by the assistant.

"Hello, Raven and Julia. Go on in. He's expecting you."

"Thank you," Raven said as they walked into Simon's office and found him sitting at a conference table with a laptop and video screen.

"Hi, Doctor," Raven said.

"Hello, Raven, Julia. I've set up the report on my laptop, so let's sit here."

Raven and Julia joined him at the conference table.

"To save time, I've separated the results of the autopsy and focused on the information concerning your mother's stomach. Is that okay?"

"Yes," Raven replied.

"I want to let you know the report is written in medical terms, so feel free to ask questions. And if either of you starts to feel queasy looking at the images, be sure to let me know."

"Thank you, Doctor, but I'll be fine," Raven replied.

"Me too," Julia said.

"Good," Simon said as he turned on the computer and brought up the video screen with a picture of Alice's dissected stomach next to a picture of another stomach. *"The stomach is on the right is from another autopsy and you can see the color is a healthy red, and the stomach lining shows no signs of ulcers or diseases. Your mother's stomach is on the left, and while there are signs of bleeding and bruising caused by the accident, there are no ulcers or other diseases that would have caused pain before the accident occurred."*

"So, what could have caused the pain?" Raven asked.

"It was most likely stomach flu."

"Or food poisoning?" Raven asked.

"Excuse me?" Simon questioned.

"Would food poisoning show up in an autopsy?"

"Only if the poison food was still in her stomach at the time of the autopsy. But her stomach was empty. But why are you asking about food poisoning?" Simon asked.

"I found a diary my mother kept, and in it, she wrote about the pain and wondered if it could have been from food poisoning."

"Did she say what she had to eat?" asked Simon, now curious.

"Just some soup and a muffin," Raven replied.

"Well, apart from examining her stomach, I also conducted a complete toxicology screening of her blood and found nothing unusual."

"Are there poisons that could be in her system and can't be detected?" Raven asked.

"Sure, there are a few. The most common one is arsenic. It dissipates from the blood after ingestion but will stay in the hair follicles or fingernails of the deceased long after death."

"For two years?"

"Possibly. But Alice wouldn't have eaten arsenic," Simon said.

"Not intentionally," Raven replied.

"Are you suggesting your mother was poisoned?" Simon asked.

Raven answers his question with one of her own. "Does arsenic cause a lot of pain?"

"Yes, an extreme amount."

"How long does it take for arsenic to take effect?"

"It depends how much is ingested. If it's a large amount, death can occur in minutes. But if it's a small amount it can take a lot longer."

"A week?" Raven asked.

"Or longer," he replied.

"Are there tests to determine if a deceased person still has arsenic in their body?" Julia asked.

"Sure, but to run them, the deceased would have to be exhumed and tested postmortem. But without proof that the person got poisoned and that the death was caused by foul play. The court would never approve the exhumation."

"Well, thank you for taking us through the report, Doctor. We appreciate it," Raven said as the two women stood up to leave.

"Should we set up a time to go through the rest of the report?" Simon asked.

"No, I've seen enough. Thank you," Raven replied, pondering what she heard.

"Listen, Raven; I'm sure stomach flu caused your mother's pain," Simon said.

"You're probably right," Raven replied as she and Julia walked out of the office.

Once the women were gone, Simon made a phone call.

"This is Doctor Simon. Can I speak to Chief Manfred? Thank you. Chief, I just finished going over the autopsy report with Raven and showed her that there was nothing wrong with Alice's stomach and that the pain her mother was experiencing was just stomach flu. But she told me that Alice kept a diary and wrote about the pain possibly *being from food poisoning. I told Raven there was no poison in the toxicology tests I ran. I'll say this, she's determined to know what happened to her mom, so I'm sure she'll come and talk to you about her suspicions, and I wanted you to be ready. No problem. Goodbye."*

When they got back to Raven's house after the meeting, Raven and Julia sat in the kitchen and looked at Alice's diary notes about her stomach pain.

"She does say the pain felt like the flu," Julia said.

"But she also wondered if it could be food poisoning. And that all she had to eat was one of Muriel's muffins and some homemade soup."

"Are you thinking Muriel put poison in the muffins she gave your mother?"

"Isn't it possible? She hated my mother because of the affair and would have wanted revenge."

"I guess it's possible," Julia said as she looked at the basket of muffins on the table. *"Did Muriel give you these?"*

"Yeah, she brought them over yesterday afternoon."

"After we met with her and the Chief?" Julia asked suspiciously.

"Yeah, why?"

"At that meeting, Muriel heard you say you're getting some of your memory back."

"That's right."

"And if you think Muriel poisoned your mother to get revenge for the affair, and she thinks you're starting to remember the accident and how it happened. That could mean-"

"Muriel wants to get rid of me, too, before I remember what really happened," Raven said as she took a muffin out of the basket and put it in a plastic bag.

"What are you doing?" Julia asked.

"I need to see the Chief. Right away," Raven replied.

"It's my turn to drive," Julia said as she followed Raven out of the house.

When they got to Police Headquarters, Julia sat in the visitor section again while Raven, carrying the bag containing the muffin, approached a police officer at the desk.

"Excuse me," Raven said as he lifted his face from the paperwork he was working on.

"Yes, miss?"

"I need to talk to Chief Manfred. It's important."

"He's in a meeting."

The Chief's office door opened at that moment, and he walked out with two other officers.

"We'll meet again this afternoon," the Chief said to the officers."

"Chief," Raven called out as she walked toward him. *"I need to talk to you."*

"Miss," the desk officer said as he tried to stop her.

"It's okay, Sergeant," the Chief said. *"What do you want, Raven? If you're here about the car re-inspection, I haven't scheduled it."*

"I'm not here about the car. I'm here to talk to you about another potential murder."

"Let's go into my office," the Chief said as Raven followed him into the office, and he shut the door. *"Now, what's this about another murder?"*

"I think Muriel murdered my mother."

"What are you talking about?" he asked, stunned.

"I found a diary my mother kept. And in it was an entry about her stomach pain getting worse. She said it felt like food poisoning."

"Okay. But what does that have to do with Muriel?"

"All my mother had to eat was one of Muriel's muffins and some soup she made herself."

"So, you think Muriel put poison in the muffin? Look, Raven. I talked to Doctor Simon, and he told me you talked to him about Alice being poisoned, but he also told you there was no poison in Alice's toxicology tests."

"That's right, he did. But he also told me that a few poisons, like arsenic, dissipate in the blood after death and can't be detected in an autopsy. But can be stored in the hair and nails of the deceased."

"Why would Muriel poison Alice?"

"For revenge. Paul told me she hated my mother for having an affair and breaking up her family, and you said she didn't take the divorce well."

"Sure. But that doesn't make her a murderer. Besides, the only proofs you have are notes in a diary and a single memory, and those aren't enough to prove murder."

"I also have this," Raven said, handing him the bag containing the muffin.

"What is this?" the Chief asked as he opened the bag.

"A muffin that Muriel gave me yesterday."

"Why bring it to me?"

"So, you can have it tested for arsenic."

"Arsenic. Why would Muriel poison you?"

"To keep me from remembering what caused the accident."

"But if she poisoned the muffins she gave you, why are you still alive?"

"I didn't eat any of them. Can you test it, please?"

"All right, I'll have it tested, but this whole thing is ridiculous. Muriel didn't poison your mother, and she's not trying to poison you."

"I hope you're right."

At that moment, there was a knock at the door, and Paul walked in. "Sorry to interrupt, sir, but I have some information concerning the Dunlap case."

"I'll call you when I have the results," the Chief said to Raven.

"Thank you, Chief. Goodbye, Paul," Raven said as she left the office.

"Goodbye, Raven," Paul replied and turned back to the Chief. "We got a tip about what happened to Dunlap."

"What do you mean?"

"The night Dunlap was murdered, there was a cleaning service inside the shop, and one of the guys said he saw a car speed out of the parking lot around the time Dunlap was killed."

"Did he see the make and color of the car?"

"Just that it was a blue SUV."

"How many blue SUVs are there in the city?"

"There's ten, including moms."

"Did the guy get a look at the car's license plate?"

"No, it was too dark, and the car was going too fast. I've pulled the names and addresses of all the owners of blue SUVs so that we can get them in and inspect them for damage."

"Good. Also, check the service records at Dunlap's on the day of Alice and Raven's accident and see if he did an oil change on Alice's car."

"Will do. Also, Chief, we got a call from Dunlap's bookkeeper asking to meet with us."

"Did he say what it was about?"

"No. He sounded nervous and said he'd tell us when he got here in about an hour."

"Listen," the Chief said as he put on his jacket. "I've got to go home and get some paperwork, but I should be back before the bookkeeper gets here. And one more thing."

"Yes, sir?"

"Raven thinks your mother murdered Alice to get revenge for our affair."

Paul's eyes widen with disbelief.

"Murdered her? How?"

"By putting arsenic in some muffins, she gave Alice."

"Does Raven have proof?"

"Just notes in a diary Alice kept, where she talked about the stomach pains, she was having to be from food poisoning and all she had to eat was a muffin Muriel gave her."

"That's ridiculous; mom wouldn't commit murder. Right?"

"I don't know; considering how much she hated me and Alice for the affair, wanting us dead wouldn't have been outside the realm of possibility."

"I don't believe it," Paul said in disbelief.

"And that's not all; Raven also thinks Muriel is trying to kill her, too."

"What? Why?"

"To stop her from remembering anything else about the accident and how Alice died. She brought me a muffin Muriel gave her to test for arsenic."

"Unbelievable," Paul said.

"I agree but keep it to yourself until we know more."

"I understand."

"Call me on my cell phone if anything comes up," the Chief said as he left the office.

"Yes, sir," Paul said.

After the Chief left, Paul paused. *"Raven, what are you doing?"*

When the Chief arrived at his house, Muriel came home from school and parked her car next to his in the garage. As the Chief got out of his police car and walked to the house entrance, he passed the front bumper of Muriel's Blue SUV and noticed it was covered with tape.

"What happened to your bumper?" the Chief asked, inspecting the dent under the tape.

"I know, terrible, isn't it? I hit a parking meter when I was out shopping," Muriel said as she got out of the car. *"You know me - I'm not as careful as I should be when I drive. I've got an appointment next week to have it fixed. Let's go in so I can start dinner,"* she said as she walked into the house.

The Chief paused and studied the dent. *"Couldn't be,"* he muttered to himself as he walked into the house. As the Chief walked in, Muriel was in the kitchen starting dinner. *"That's a pretty bad dent. When did it happen?"*

"Yesterday. I went shopping after our meeting."

"Did you knock over the parking meter when you hit it?"

"No, the meter was fine," Muriel said, smiling. "My bumper took all the damage. You know these cheap foreign cars."

"Yeah. Well, I'm glad you weren't hurt. I can't stay for dinner; I got to get back to the station," the Chief said as he picked up a folder off the dining room table. "Herman's bookkeeper is coming to the station to talk to us."

"About what?"

"Don't know, but it must have something to do with Herman's finances, which could potentially shed some light on a motive for his murder."

"That's good. Listen, if you won't be here for dinner, I think I'll go out go and get something."

"Good idea. I'll see you later," he said and left.

When the Chief got back to his office, Paul and another older man waited for him outside his office door.

"Chief, this is Milton Millsap," Paul said. "He's been Herman's bookkeeper for the last twenty years."

"Nice meeting you, Milton," the Chief said as he shook Milton's hand. "Let's go into my office."

He unlocked the office door, and the three men walked into the office and sat at the conference table.

"Tell the Chief what you were telling me," Paul said to Milton.

"Yes, please," the Chief said.

"First off," Milton said shyly, "I want you to know that I liked Herman and was upset when he died."

"We all were," replied the Chief.

"But he wasn't a good businessman. He was going bankrupt and was desperate to find the cash to save his business."

"How much did he need?" the Chief asked.

"Seventy-five thousand dollars. His bank told him that if he didn't have the money by the end of last August, they were going to seize his property and shut him down."

"He must have gotten the money somehow. The shop was still open," Paul said.

"Yeah, he got the money, but he never told me where. But when he was killed, I started to wonder if the money had something to do with it."

"And you don't know who gave him the money?" the Chief asked.

"All he said was that it was from a customer he did some work for that wanted to help save the business."

"A customer, huh? Well, we appreciate you coming in and talking to us, Milton," the Chief said as he stood up. *"You've certainly given us some valuable information."*

"I just wish I could have done something to save Herman's life," Milton said as he stood up to leave.

"If you think of anything else, don't hesitate to call us," the Chief said as Milton left the office.

"What do you think?" the Chief asked Paul.

"I think whoever gave Herman the money wanted something from him in return."

"Yeah, but what? Did you check to see if Alice brought her car to Dunlap for an oil change the morning of the accident?"

"She did. According to the business service records, Alice brought her car in at around nine, got an oil change, and then left at eleven."

As the Chief pondered what Paul told him about the oil change, his office phone rang, and he answered it.

"This is Chief Manfred. ...What? Are you sure? ... Thanks," the Chief hung up the phone and looked at Paul.

"The muffins Muriel gave you do contain arsenic" he said, shocked.

"Oh my God!" Paul exclaimed. "She is trying to kill Raven."

"And that means she also killed Alice, and unless I miss my guess Dunlap, too," the Chief said his lip twitching.

"Why do you say that?" Paul asked.

"I saw a dent in the front bumper of your mother's blue SUV. She said it happened when she hit a parking meter, but she was lying. Get over to our house and bring your mother and her car back here so we can talk to her. I'll call Raven and let her know about the arsenic," the Chief said.

"Yes, sir," Paul replied, preparing to leave.

"And, son," the Chief said, halting him in his tracks.

"Even though she's your mother, be careful."

"I will," Paul said and walked out of the office.

After the meeting with the Chief, Raven was at home sitting at the kitchen table having coffee and looking through Alice's diary again.

"You and the Chief were in love, weren't you, Mom?" Raven said as she looked at one of the diary pages. *"And I know Muriel hated you for it and killed you to get revenge."*

She flipped to another page and went glassy-eyed as another memory flashed through her mind.

In the memory, Raven and Alice were sitting in the car's front seat, on their way to drop Raven back at college. Raven could see Alice holding the steering wheel with both hands, concentrating on her driving and driving at a steady pace, and not speeding. Raven could see the car was on the highway next to a cliff, and the weather was clear.

"A senior in college! I'm so proud of you, Raven," Alice said as she reached over and held Raven's hand.

"Thank you, Mom. This means that at the end of this year, I'll be a high school art teacher just like you."

"No, not like me, you'll be way better than me. Listen, Raven. There's something important I need to tell you."

"What is it, Mom?"

"Last year, while you were away at school, I had an...."

Before she finished her sentence, Alice winced in severe pain, let go of the steering wheel, and clutched her stomach.

"Ow!" Alice screamed.

Raven watched in terror as the car swerved off the road toward the cliff.

"Mom, watch out!"

Alice fought through the pain, grabbed the steering wheel, and guided the car back on the road.

"Mom, are you okay?"

"No," Alice shrieked as the pain erupted again, and she let go of the steering wheel again and doubled over. As the car drifted off the road toward the cliff again, Raven grabbed the wheel and tried to steer it back on the road.

"Put the brakes on, Mom," Raven yelled.

Alice again fought the pain and stepped on the brakes, but they failed to engage. Realizing they couldn't stop the car from going over the cliff, the two terrified women reached for one another, and as their hands touched, the car sailed over the cliff, and the memory faded.

"Oh my god, the brakes didn't work," Raven exclaimed. "And it was the stomach pain from the arsenic Muriel gave her that caused my mother to lose control of the car."

At that very moment, the phone rang, and Raven rushed to answer it.

"Hello."

"Raven, it's Chief Manfred. It's confirmed. The muffins Muriel gave you contain arsenic."

"I knew it."

"Paul is trying to locate Muriel now, but she could show up at your house."

"What should I do?"

"If she shows up, try not to let her into the house. I'll send an officer over."

"Thank you, Chief. Goodbye."

As Raven set the phone down, the doorbell rang. Raven nervously peered through the peephole and saw Muriel standing on the porch. Raven stepped away from the door, and Muriel kept ringing the bell. When the bell finally stopped, Raven looked through the peephole and didn't see Muriel. Raven moved away from the door and looked out a front window. Not seeing a car parked in front of the house, Raven she went back to the front door, opened it slightly, and didn't see Muriel.

"She must have left," Raven said as Muriel appeared in front of her.

"Ah, Raven. You are home, after all. Didn't you hear the bell?"

"No, I was in the bathroom, sorry."

"Can I come in?" Muriel asked as she pushed past Raven without waiting for an answer and walked into the house, locking the door behind her.

"It's good to see you, Muriel, but why are you here?" Raven asked, trying to remain calm.

"I just came over to see how you're doing," Muriel said, walking into the living room and sitting on the couch.

"I'm doing fine," Raven replied. "Would you like a cup of coffee?"

"No, thank you. I can't stay. Sit down." Muriel said and indicated for Raven to sit next to her on the couch.

As Raven sat down, Muriel stopped talking and stared at her with a menacing look. "The meeting with the Chief yesterday was quite *interesting, wasn't it?"*

"What do you mean?" Raven asked, playing coy.

"Well, you learned a lot. You found out your mother's old car is still at the impound and that it can be inspected again."

"Yes, I didn't expect that."

"And you raised suspicions about the validity of Herman's accident report."

"True, but I won't have proof until they reinspect the car."

"You also got permission to review Alice's autopsy report."

"That's right."

"And? Have you gone through it yet?"

"Yes."

"Lovely. Did you find out what caused Alice's stomach pain?" Muriel asked, opening her handbag.

"The doctor said that it was the stomach flu, and that's why it didn't show up in the autopsy."

"Interesting. How about your memory? Have any more memories of the accident?" Muriel asked, continuing to stare.

Raven paused. "No, just the one I told you about."

"Are you sure? You didn't remember your mother thought her stomach pain could have been from food poisoning?"

Fraught with anxiety, Raven starts to stand up.

"She was wrong; it was stomach flu after all."

"Is that right?" Muriel said as she pulled Raven back down on the couch. "Going somewhere?" she said as she grabbed Raven's arm and held her down.

Fearing for her life, Raven tried talking to Muriel, "Look, Muriel, I know about the affair the Chief had with my mother. But according to him, you two were going through a divorce when he started seeing my mother."

"Huh. So, you know about that? I'm not surprised. Listen to me - Alice was supposed to be my friend, and she knew I was trying to reconcile with the Chief, and yet, she still kept seeing him."

"Yes, but she felt guilty about it."

"That's bullshit. The bitch didn't even have the guts to tell me about the affair herself."

"Is that why you put arsenic in the muffins you gave her? To get revenge?"

"What are you talking about? That's a baseless accusation, you can't prove I put arsenic in the muffins, the toxicology report found nothing in her system."

"That's right, but arsenic can stay in the body after death. So, if her body is exhumed and tested, I know it will be there."

"You know that will never happen, it requires proof of foul play, and you don't have it."

"No, but I do have the muffins you gave me, and according to the Chief, they contain arsenic."

Muriel smiles, her eyes full of malice. *"Why couldn't you have died in the accident like your mother? Then no one would have ever known what I did. But now, I can't let you remember anything else,"* Muriel said as she took a muffin and a gun out of her purse and pointed the gun at Raven. *"This time, I'll make sure you eat the muffin,"* Muriel said.

"Haven't you damaged my life enough already?"

"Like you and your mother damaged mine?" Muriel yelled, hysterical. *"Besides, I don't have a choice. Without you, they can't prove anything. It'll all be circumstantial. Remember, I'm a cop's wife. I know how the law works. You could have put the arsenic in the muffins you gave my husband to frame me."*

"What about Dunlap? Did you kill him too?"

"You made me do it. When you remembered the oil change, he got scared the police would find out that he adjusted the brakes on your mother's car and tell them I paid him to do it."

"You won't get away with this; the police are on their way here right now," Raven said.

"Then you better eat fast," Muriel said as she held out the muffin.

At that moment, the doorbell rang.

"That's the police," Raven said, pushing the muffin away.

"No. If they thought I was here, they wouldn't ring the doorbell," Muriel said as she walked over to the door, looked out the peephole, and saw Julia standing on the porch.

"It's your little friend Julia. Shall we invite her in to join the party?" Muriel said, holding up the gun threateningly.

"Don't hurt her; she didn't do anything wrong," Raven whispered angrily.

Julia rang the bell a few more times and tried to open the door. Finding it locked, Julia walked off the porch, and Muriel made her way back to Raven.

"Stop stalling and eat the fucking muffin. And don't worry, I put so much arsenic in it, you'll die fast."

"But when the police get here and find me dead, what are you going to tell them?"

"That you were mentally distraught and contemplating suicide and called me for help. And when I got here, you tried to poison me with arsenic you slipped into a coffee you served me to get revenge for what you thought I did to Alice. But when I realized what you were doing, we fought, and I forced you to drink the poisoned coffee in self-defense. Now for the last time, take a bite of the muffin," Muriel said as she brought the muffin closer to Raven's face.

Desperate, Raven kicked Muriel in the stomach with her prosthesis, and she dropped the gun and the muffin and fell to the floor. Raven got up from the couch and reached for the gun, but Muriel got to it first and stood up.

"I guess you'd rather die from a bullet. So be it," Muriel said as she cocked the trigger on the gun.

"Wait," Raven yelled out frantically. "You don't have to kill me. I'll say I was wrong about you."

"Nice try, but it's too late for that," Muriel said and put her finger on the trigger.

But before she could fire, Julia ran into the living room from the hallway and jumped on Muriel.

"You're not going to kill anyone else, you bitch," Julia yelled angrily as she and Muriel wrestled for the gun. Tugging wildly, Muriel was able to get the gun away from Julia.

"This is perfect, now I can tie up all the loose ends at the same time," Muriel said as she fired a shot and hit Julia in the side.

Julia screamed and fell to the floor, passed out, and Raven ran over to her.

"You're a sick fucking monster," Raven screamed at Muriel as she held Julia.

As Muriel picked up the muffin and turned her attention back to Raven, a police siren was heard coming up the street.

"That is the police. So, let's make this quick," Muriel said as she tried to force Raven to take a bite of the muffin.

Struggling to keep the muffin away from her, Raven pushed Muriel away and grabbed the gun out of her hand.

"Back the fuck off," Raven said and fired a shot that hit Muriel in the leg. As Muriel dropped the muffin and fell to the floor screaming in pain, Raven heard Paul's voice on the porch.

"Mom are you in there?" he shouted as he tried to open the door.

"Help" Raven screamed.

Paul forced the front door open, rushed in with his gun drawn, and saw his mother lying on the floor and Raven standing over her with the gun in her hand.

"Paul, she's trying to kill me," Muriel shrieked.

"She's lying, Paul," Raven replied. *"You know what she's trying to do."*

"Drop the gun, Raven," Paul said.

"But, Paul," Raven said as she hesitated to drop the gun.

"Please, Raven, you don't need to be afraid; I'm here, now," Paul said.

Raven dropped the gun on the floor and ran back to Julia while Paul walked over to pick up the gun. Before he got to it, Muriel rolled over, grabbed the gun, and pointed the barrel at her own head.

"Mom, what are you doing?"

"I can't let you arrest me. I'll spend the rest of my life in jail. This is all your Mother's fault" Muriel said to Raven as she cocked the trigger.

"Mom, don't shoot. We can work this out, I promise," Paul said, trying to distract her.

"You're such a sweet boy, Paul, and I love you so much, but there's nothing to work out. Because of your father and Alice, my life, our life, was ruined, and I won't live out the rest of it behind bars," she said.

As Muriel starts to pull the trigger, Paul rushes over, grabs the gun, and pulls it away from her.

"No, I won't let you kill yourself," he said as he bent down next to her. *"I'll never understand or condone what you did, and you might spend the rest of your life in jail. But I'll be there to help."*

Muriel smiles with tears streaming down her cheeks, picks up the muffin, and takes a bite. *"It's better this way, son. Trust me. And take care of your father and tell him I always loved him."*

Almost immediately, Muriel writhed in pain from the arsenic and started to pass out.

"Mom, don't worry, I'll get you to the hospital," Paul said and turned to Raven.

"Are you okay?" Paul said to Raven.

"Yes, thanks to you."

"How's Julia?" Paul asked.

"She's lost a lot of blood and needs to get to the hospital," Raven replied.

At that moment, ambulance and police sirens are heard in front of the house.

"On my way over, I called for back-up. Just in case," Paul said and walked back to Muriel.

"Hang on, Mom, the ambulance is here to take you to the hospital," Paul said as two ambulance attendants walked into the house with stretchers.

"The Chief is on the way, Sergeant."

"Thank you, officer," Paul said. *"Let's get them both to the hospital."*

One attendant walked over to Muriel and checked her pulse.

"I'm sorry, sir, but she's passed away."

Paul walked to his mother's body. *"Why, Mom? Why did you do it?*

I love you. You can take her out," he said to the attendant, his eyes downcast and pained.

"What about Julia?" Raven asked. *"Is she going to be okay?"*

"Fuck yes, I'll be okay," Julia said weakly, regaining consciousness. *"You still need more driving lessons."*

"You saved my life," Raven said to Julia as the attendant placed her on the stretcher. *"But how did you know I needed help?"*

"I saw Muriel through the window holding a gun on you. So, I picked the lock on the back door."

"We need to go," the ambulance attendant said as he wheeled her out of the house.

"I'll see you at the hospital," Raven said to Julia as she and Paul followed Julia and Muriel out of the house.

As the attendants put Julia and Muriel into the ambulances, the Chief drove up, got out of his police car, and walked over to Paul.

"What happened?" the Chief asked.

"Julia stopped Mom from shooting Raven and got shot herself."

"Is she all right?" the Chief asked.

"I hope so," replied Raven.

"And Muriel?" the Chief asked.

"She didn't make it, Dad. She ate an arsenic muffin she brought for Raven and killed herself."

"I'm so sorry about Muriel, Chief," Raven said.

For a moment, his face was grim. But then, the Chief responded, *"Don't be. She murdered your mother and tried to kill you. I'm the one who should be sorry. I should have realized Muriel never got over the affair and how upset she was when you came back and started to remember things. And I owe you an apology, too, son. This whole thing is my fault. As much as I loved Alice, if I hadn't brought her into this, both she and Muriel would still be alive."*

"It's not all your fault, Dad. I knew Mom was angry about the affair too, but I never thought she would resort to murder to get revenge."

"Raven, are you able to come to the station and give us a statement?" the Chief asked.

"Yes," Raven said.

"I'll bring her," Paul said.

"Good. Then I'll see you both at the station. I'm going with Muriel," the Chief said, getting into Muriel's ambulance as it drove off.

"Ready to go?" Paul asked Raven.

"Yeah. Can we stop at the hospital so I can check on Julia?"

"Sure."

Paul and Raven got in his patrol car and drove off.

"How are you feeling?" Raven asked.

"I don't know yet. I still can't believe my mother was a murderer."

"The whole thing shouldn't have happened," Raven replied. *"How did you know Muriel would come after me?"*

"Once we knew the muffin she gave you contained arsenic, we figured she wouldn't stop until you were dead."

"Muriel admitted to me that she was the one who paid Dunlap to make the brakes fail on my mother's car and that she killed him to keep him from talking."

"Yeah. We found Dunlap's DNA on the front bumper of her car. And his accountant told us that Dunlap needed seventy-five-thousand dollars to save his business, and my mother gave him the money to fix the brakes and lie on his inspection report."

"Where did she get the money, she gave Dunlap?"

"From her savings, but we're verifying that with her bank."

"I remembered how the accident happened. The stomach pain from the arsenic Muriel gave my mother caused her to lose control of the car."

"I'm so sorry," Paul said remorsefully.

"And I'm sorry, too. Both our mothers are dead, and my mother should have stopped the affair."

"Yeah, my dad, too."

They arrived at the hospital, and before they got out of the car, Raven looked at Paul.

"Thank you again, Paul, for saving my life. And once we're both feeling better, I'd like to take you up on your offer to have dinner. If your fiancée is okay with it?"

"She won't have a problem; she broke off our engagement."

"Oh, I'm sorry. Why?"

"She suspected I still had feelings for you."

"Is she right?" Raven asked, smiling.

Paul leaned over and kissed her tenderly.

"What was that for," Raven asked.

"To answer your question."

THE END

www.ingramcontent.com/pod-product-compliance
Lightning Source LLC
Chambersburg PA
CBHW022042170626
46808CB00003B/1333